Sometimes When I'm Sad

Deborah Serani, Psy.D.
illustrated by Kyra Teis

free spirit
PUBLISHING®

Library of Congress Cataloging-in-Publication Data
Names: Serani, Deborah, 1961- author. | Teis, Kyra, illustrator.
Title: Sometimes when I'm sad / by Deborah Serani ; illustrated by Kyra Teis.
Description: Minneapolis, MN : Free Spirit Publishing Inc., [2020] | Audience: Ages 4–8 |
Identifiers: LCCN 2019031721 (print) | LCCN 2019031722 (ebook) | ISBN 9781631983825 (hardcover) |
    ISBN 9781631983832 (pdf) | ISBN 9781631983849 (epub)
Subjects: LCSH: Sadness—Juvenile literature. | Depression in children—Diagnosis—Juvenile literature.
Classification: LCC RJ506.D4 S465 2020 (print) | LCC RJ506.D4 (ebook) | DDC 618.92/8527—dc23
LC record available at https://lccn.loc.gov/2019031721
LC ebook record available at https://lccn.loc.gov/2019031722

Free Spirit Publishing does not have control over or assume responsibility for author or third-party websites and their content.

Reading Level Grade 2; Interest Level Ages 4–8
Fountas & Pinnell Guided Reading Level M

Edited by Alison Behnke
Cover and interior design by Emily Dyer

10 9 8 7 6 5 4 3 2 1
Printed in China
R18860120

Free Spirit Publishing Inc.
6325 Sandburg Road, Suite 100
Minneapolis, MN 55427-3674
(612) 338-2068
help4kids@freespirit.com
freespirit.com

FSC
www.fsc.org
MIX
Paper from
responsible sources
FSC® C144853

Free Spirit offers competitive pricing.
Contact edsales@freespirit.com for pricing information on multiple quantity purchases.

For Nicole

Sometimes when I'm sad, I cry.

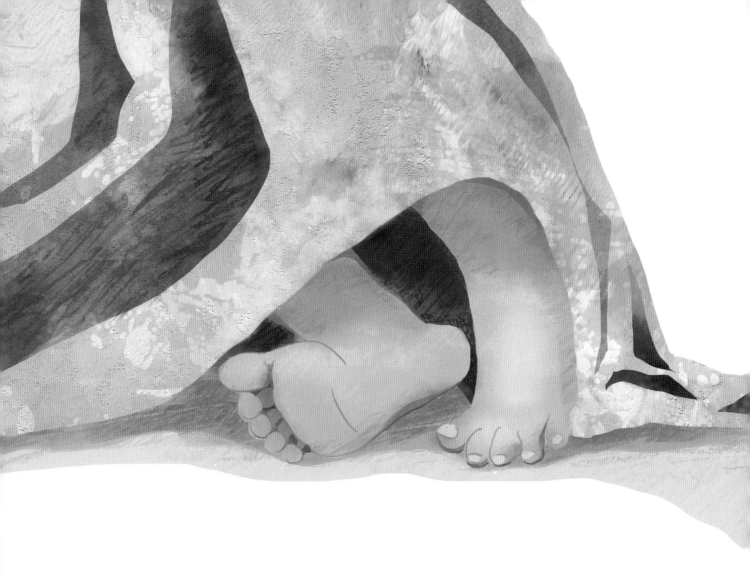

Sometimes I hide.

Sometimes I even throw my toys.

Sometimes when I'm sad,
nothing helps me feel happy.

Not even presents.

Or ice cream.

Or a basket full of bunnies.

Sometimes when I'm sad,
I want to sleep all day.

Or just sit on the couch
doing nothing at all.

One day,
I met a counselor.

She helps children learn about feelings.

She said sometimes sadness can get so big that it takes up all the space where happiness should be.

So I learned how to make
my sad feelings smaller.

She told me
it's okay to cry.

It's okay to hide,

but not for a long time.

She said if the sadness won't go away,
I can talk about it.

With a grown-up
who loves me.

With my friends.

Or with her.

I learned that I can draw
the sadness I feel with crayons.

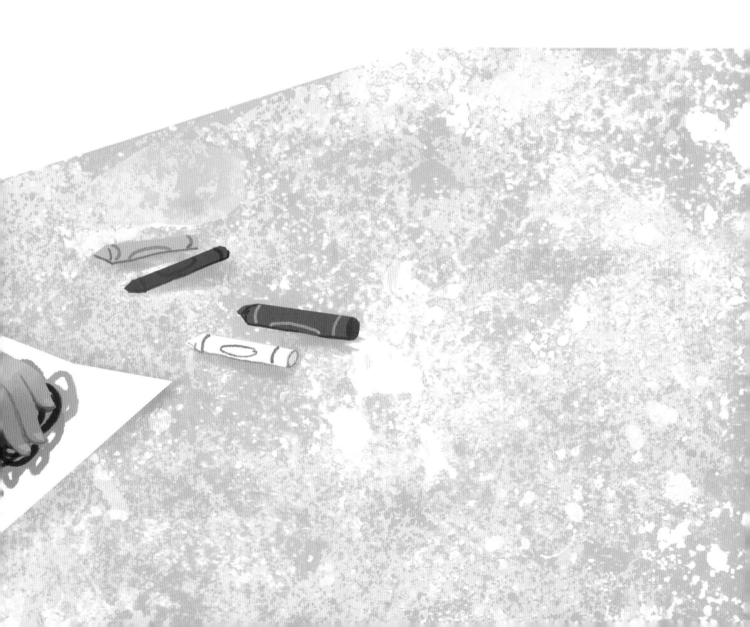

Instead of throwing my toys,
I can throw a ball really hard.

I can run and
jump outside.

I can squish and squash clay.

Holding something soft or warm can help me feel better.

So can listening to nice sounds, like rain falling, birds singing, or music I love.

Or sniffing a good smell,
like flowers, fruit,
or fresh air.

Or tasting
healthy food.

Even spending time with nature
can make sadness go away.

So I tried a lot of these things.

And she was right.

Now when I get sad,
I still cry sometimes.

And I still hide sometimes.

But only for a little while.

Because now I know
ways to feel better.

HELPING CHILDREN THROUGH SADNESS
A Guide for Caring Adults

The theme of this book is sadness in childhood. We all know that children get sad, and that sadness can be experienced differently by each child. Additionally, young children experience sadness in different ways than older children, teenagers, or adults. Because they don't have the language or cognitive development to express sadness verbally, it often reveals itself in less obvious ways. For instance, children may complain about aches and pains, hide or isolate themselves, and express irritability, anger, or fatigue. This is why it may be hard for caring adults to see and recognize the symptoms of sadness.

Sometimes, a sad feeling is more than simple sadness. It may become a daily occurrence and might linger for days, weeks, or even months. This persistent kind of sadness is not just a passing phase and could be a sign of pediatric depression. It's estimated that in the United States alone, 1 percent of infants, 4 percent of preschool-age children, and 5 percent of school-age children meet the criteria for major depression. Learning the unique behavioral and physical symptoms of sadness in children can help you prevent a clinical disorder from developing. By reading *Sometimes When I'm Sad* with a child or a group of children, you'll learn and teach about the textures of sadness as well as how to deal with the emotion when it occurs.

HOW TO SPOT SADNESS IN CHILDREN OF DIFFERING AGES

Sadness can look different in children of varying ages. And while every individual child experiences and demonstrates emotions in unique ways, certain patterns and common expressions do exist. These can help you become aware of sadness in children you care for, and in turn can help you support them in coping with their feelings.

Infants: Babies who experience sadness may have a weak cry, show poor appetite, appear lethargic, and demonstrate a slow eye gaze when looking at faces, objects, or their own reflection. They may also show disinterest in toys or in socializing with others and may occasionally be difficult to soothe. Often, babies struggling with sadness are delayed in achieving developmental milestones such as sitting up, reaching for objects, and babbling.

Toddlers: Two- and three-year-olds who experience sadness are highly sensitive and easily hurt, which can lead to tearfulness, crying, or anger. This hypersensitivity occurs because children this age don't have the language and cognitive skills to fully express their sad feelings. The sadness is experienced as an irritability on an emotional level, which can frequently be challenging and overwhelming for children this age. Sadness can affect toddlers in physical ways too. Many children complain about aches and pains such as stomachaches, headaches, earaches, and the like when they are feeling sad.

Preschool-age children: With greater access to language than toddlers and infants, most preschool children can express themselves with words. However, their use of language does not always accurately or clearly reflect the sadness they feel. Be on the lookout for phrases like, *"I'm so mad," "This is stupid,"* or *"I hate this."* Also watch for behaviors such as breaking things, clinging, sulking, or isolating themselves from others. These are more common ways preschoolers experience and express sadness. In children of all ages, sadness seeps into the body, so preschoolers feeling sadness will frequently be tired, whiny, or fussy. They may also complain about aches and pains.

School-age children: Children this age are generally more skilled in expressing their emotions than younger children. Some may be able to communicate sadness by using language like, *"I'm feeling sad," "This makes me feel bad,"* or *"I'm upset."* But others might struggle in both detecting sadness and communicating it. School-age children may look glum or appear quiet, or they may display opposite behaviors like argumentativeness, irritability, and impatience. Other signs of sadness include a decreased level of energy, working slowly to finish schoolwork or other tasks (at school or at home), and poor concentration, as well as a lack of interest in games and toys, playing with friends, or doing other activities. Eating too much or too little can be a sign of sadness in these children, as can changes in sleeping patterns. Like other age ranges, school-age children experience aches and pains as a result of feeling sad.

WAYS TO REDUCE SADNESS IN CHILDREN

Once you've identified the unique ways children experience sadness, there are many approaches you can take to help them reduce their sad feelings. A good guideline is to use the five senses to revitalize a child's mind and body. Sadness is often an experience of depletion, in which emotions are flattened or weakened. Sadness also diminishes children physically, creating weariness and fatigue. By feeding the senses, we not only connect with children, we bring evidenced-based comfort into our approach.

Sight: The sun and natural light hold powerful benefits for reducing sadness. Invite natural light into your classroom, home, or workspace. Open any shades, curtains, or blinds. Allow children of all ages to play or rest in the outdoor light—or in a pool of sunlight indoors. Consider incorporating color into the environment. Bright, vivid, and deeply rich colors can improve moods. You might bring these hues into your space through pictures, bulletin board backgrounds, paint colors, decorations, age-appropriate objects (such as stuffed animals, toys, and mobiles), or even clothing. Rotate new colors in and old ones out so the environment doesn't get stale. Also invite children to play with color by using coloring books, paint sets, blocks, or clay.

Additionally, it can be powerful to welcome nature into children's world and help them experience the discovery of color and texture, be it in the form of leaves, flowers, animals, water, earth, or sky. Hold a leaf for an infant to explore. Have a toddler sort rocks of different colors. Ask older children what they see in the clouds above.

Smell: Open the windows when possible to allow fresh air to circulate. Doing so brings negative ions into the room, which helps reduce sadness. You might consider using ionic air filters to clean indoor air if open windows aren't a safe or realistic option. Sadness in children can also be reduced by introducing pleasant natural smells into the environment, such as lavender, lemon, orange, or patchouli or peppermint. *Aromatherapy*, which is the use of scents to boost healing and comfort, can lift mood, improve concentration, and lessen fatigue. Use potpourri, stick diffusers, or a cool spray diffuser with essential oils to enhance the scents in your space. If allergies aren't an issue, fresh flowers and green plants are a great way to bring the outside world indoors and scrub-clean the air. Another approach that engages the sense of smell is deep breathing, a technique that provides ease and peacefulness. Often called *tummy breathing* or *belly breath*, this strategy is easy to teach to children through seven simple steps:

1. Sit down.
2. Close your eyes if you feel comfortable and safe doing so.
3. Place your hands on your belly.
4. With your mouth closed, take a big breath through your nose until you feel your belly fill up.
5. Hold that breath and silently say your name to yourself in your mind.
6. Now let the breath out slowly through your mouth.
7. Do it all again one more time!

Taste: Teaching children to embrace their sense of taste increases happiness. Encourage them to appreciate and savor a variety of flavors and textures. Invite children to linger on something sweet, savory, and salty and think about or describe the taste of each. Coach children to experience the crunch of a carrot, the crisp bite of an apple, the smooth creaminess of a cube of cheese, the warmth of hot cocoa, or the melty coldness of homemade fruit ice pops. Certain foods can also lift mood, so children who are sad can benefit from eating healthily. Foods like lean meat (including chicken, turkey, and some cuts of pork) and omega-rich fish and eggs are excellent choices. Multigrain breads, leafy greens, granola, nuts, and citrus fruits are also positive choices. These foods regulate blood sugar levels, which brings about greater physical well-being. Typical comfort foods like soup, yogurt, and warm milk can be great mood lifters for children too. While it's tempting to give a child who is sad a sweet treat, it's best to avoid foods that are high in sugar, like most candy, ice cream, soda, or juices. These spike blood sugar levels, which results in irritability and mood swings. Teach children that reaching for healthful foods nurtures their bodies and their minds.

Touch: Exercise and soothing touches reduce sadness. These activities reduce the stress hormone *cortisol* and increase the feel-good hormone *oxytocin*. Encourage exercise and movement through play, dance, sports, or other structured or semi-structured activities. Briefer and more spontaneous physical moments like holding a beloved pet, enjoying the softness of a blanket or the velvety feel of a stuffed animal, getting a hug from a trusted adult like a parent or teacher, or holding hands with a friend are also instant mood lifters. Consider helping children become familiar with textures through tactile experiences such as tending to the plants in class, a school garden, or in a garden at home. Finger-painting, cooking, building things, and other moments that involve touch and creativity are excellent activities for children who are sad. Weighted blankets and toys can also soothe children. At home, invite calming experiences like warm baths.

Hearing: Listening to relaxing sounds produces *theta waves*—brain waves that bring a state of calm and peace. When listening to nature soundscapes like the ocean, a light rain, babbling brooks, or forest sounds, children can experience theta waves and feel their sadness soothed. Similarly, classical music in major keys (not minor) reduces sadness. Teach children not only to hear, but to listen—focusing on the deep tones or soothing pitches of sounds in their environment. An open window or a walk outside can bring sounds of nature. Birds singing. Leaves scattering. Rain falling. Reading a book aloud to children can help them appreciate different sounds of voices. Listening to silly songs or funny stories also lifts mood. Laughter has long been shown to be stress reliever, reduce pain, ease sadness, and strengthen the immune system (to name just a few of its many benefits). Finally, consider teaching a child who struggles with sadness that silence can bring its own comfort. Model this by being present but quiet with the child, sitting nearby, perhaps holding a hand—or simply remaining in a quiet moment with a smile or a deep breath.

WHEN TO SEEK PROFESSIONAL HELP

Now that you know the symptoms of sadness at different age levels, as well as ways to reduce sad feelings, you can begin to help children. Using these tips and techniques should bring some immediate relief to a child struggling with sadness. This means that within a day or two, you can expect that the child will display fewer symptoms of sadness, both physical and emotional. If, however, symptoms of sadness are slower to reduce—or if they return a week or so later—it may be time to seek a consultation with a mental health or medical professional. A more formal evaluation will determine if the sadness a child is experiencing is the clinical disorder called *pediatric depression*. If a depressive disorder is occurring, proper treatment can help children heal and lead meaningful, healthy, productive lives.

RESOURCES FOR MORE INFORMATION AND SUPPORT

Mental Health

Anxiety and Depression Association of America adaa.org

Canadian Mental Health Association cmha.ca

Child Mind Institute childmind.org

Depression and Bipolar Support Alliance dbsalliance.org

Families for Depression Awareness familyaware.org

International Foundation for Research and Education on Depression ifred.org

Mental Health America mentalhealthamerica.net

National Alliance on Mental Illness nami.org

National Institute of Mental Health nimh.nih.gov

World Association for Infant Mental Health waimh.org

Parenting

Healthy Child Care America (American Academy of Pediatrics) healthychildcare.org

National Federation of Families for Children's Mental Health ffcmh.org

National Foster Parent Association nfpaonline.org

National Parenting Education Network npen.org

National Parent Help Line nationalparenthelpline.org

855-4A PARENT (855-427-2736)

National PTA pta.org

Suicide Prevention and Awareness

American Foundation for Suicide Prevention afsp.org

American Association of Suicidology suicidology.org

Centre for Suicide Prevention (Canada) suicideinfo.ca

National Suicide Prevention Lifeline suicidepreventionlifeline.org

800-273-TALK (800-273-8255)

Suicide Prevention International spiorg.org

ABOUT THE AUTHOR AND ILLUSTRATOR

Deborah Serani, Psy.D., is an award-winning author and psychologist who has been in practice for thirty years. She is also a professor at Adelphi University. Dr. Serani is a go-to expert for psychological issues. Her writing on depression and trauma has been published in many academic journals, and her interviews can be found in *Newsday*, *Psychology Today*, *The Chicago Tribune*, *The New York Times*, *The Associated Press*, and affiliate radio programs at CBS and NPR, among others. She is also a TEDx speaker. Dr. Serani lives on Long Island, New York.

Kyra Teis is a children's book author-illustrator, a graphic novelist, and an avid sewer of costumes and clothing. She works in a cozy studio in central New York, which is crammed full of books and fabrics from all over the world. When she's not making art, you can find her and her husband cheering wildly at their two daughters' soccer games and musical theater productions.

Other Great Books from Free Spirit

I'm Happy-Sad Today
Making Sense of Mixed-Together Feelings
by Lory Britain, Ph.D., illustrated by Matthew Rivera
For ages 3–8. 40 pp.; HC; color illust.; 11¼" x 9¼".

1–2–3 My Feelings and Me
by Goldie Millar and Lisa A. Berger, illustrated by Priscilla Burris
For ages 3–8. 40 pp.; HC; color illust.; 11¼" x 9¼".

F Is for Feelings
by Goldie Millar and Lisa A. Berger, illustrated by Hazel Mitchell
For ages 3–8. 40 pp.; PB and HC; color illust.; 11¼" x 9¼".

ABC Ready for School
An Alphabet of Social Skills
by Celeste C. Delaney, illustrated by Stephanie Fizer Coleman
For ages 3–6. 40 pp.; HC; color illust.; 11¼" x 9¼".

Gentle Hands and Other Sing-Along Songs for Social-Emotional Learning
by Amadee Ricketts, illustrated by Ashley Barron
For ages 3–8. 32 pp.; HC; color illust.; 11¼" x 9¼"; includes downloadable sheet music for all songs.

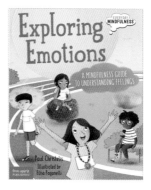

Exploring Emotions
A Mindfulness Guide to Understanding Feelings
by Paul Christelis, illustrated by Elisa Paganelli
For ages 5–9. 32 pp; HC; color illust.; 7½" x 9".

Free Leader's Guide
freespirit.com/leader